For my family
And all our years down the Shore

Clarion Books
a Houghton Mifflin Company imprint
215 Park Avenue South, New York, NY 10003
Copyright © 2006 by David Wiesner

The illustrations were executed in watercolor.
The text was set in Regula & Escrita.
Title-page lettering by David Wiesner.
Art direction by Carol Goldenberg.

ISBN-13: 978-0-618-19457-5
ISBN-10: 0-618-19457-6

Full cataloging information is available from the Library of Congress.

TWP 10 9
4500320433

FLOTSAM

DAVID WIESNER

CLARION BOOKS · NEW YORK

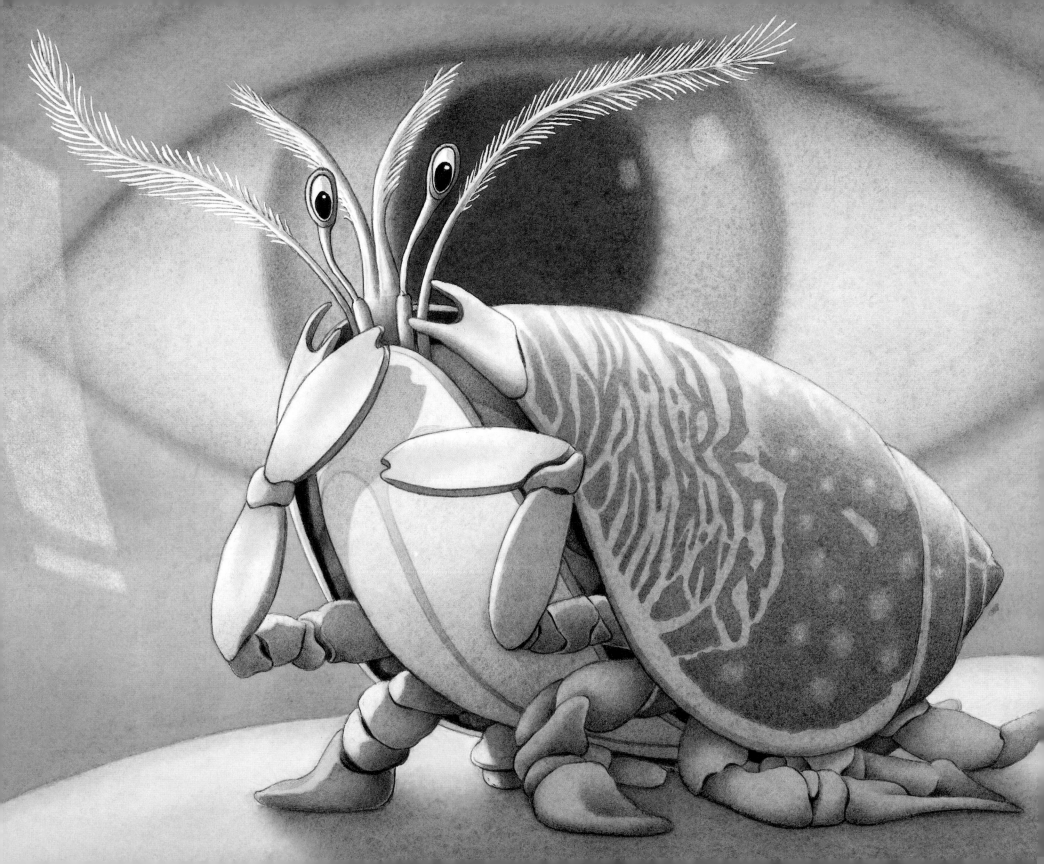

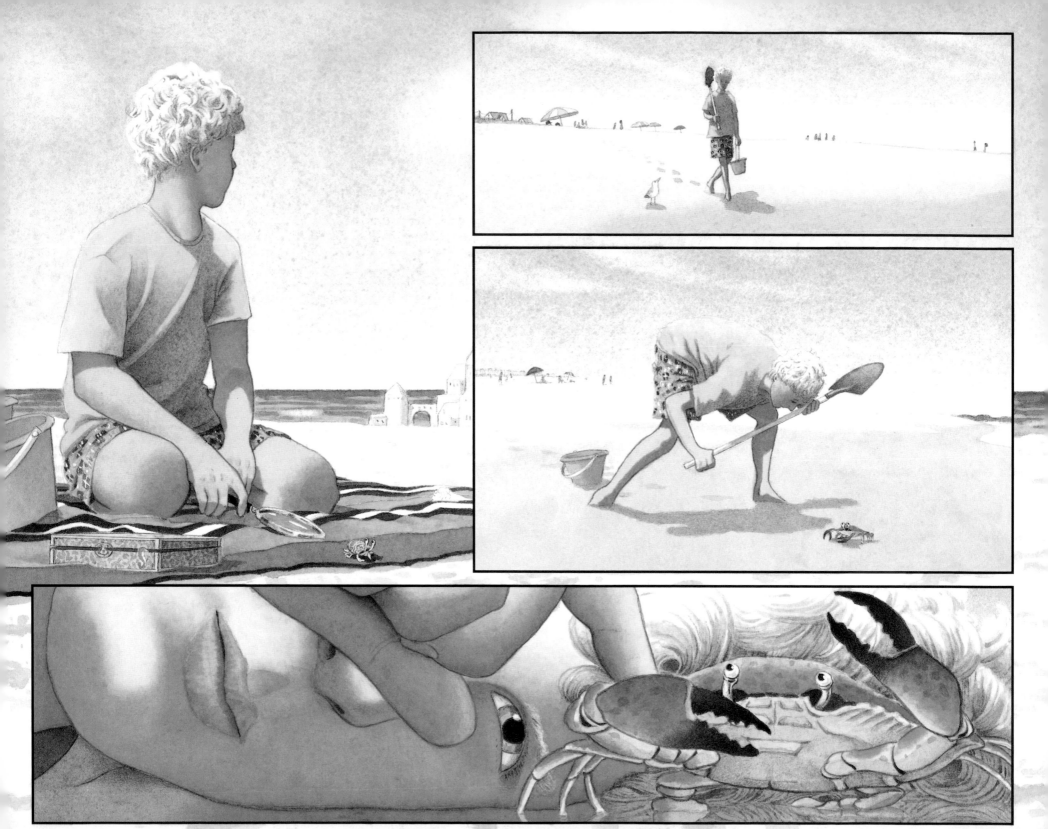

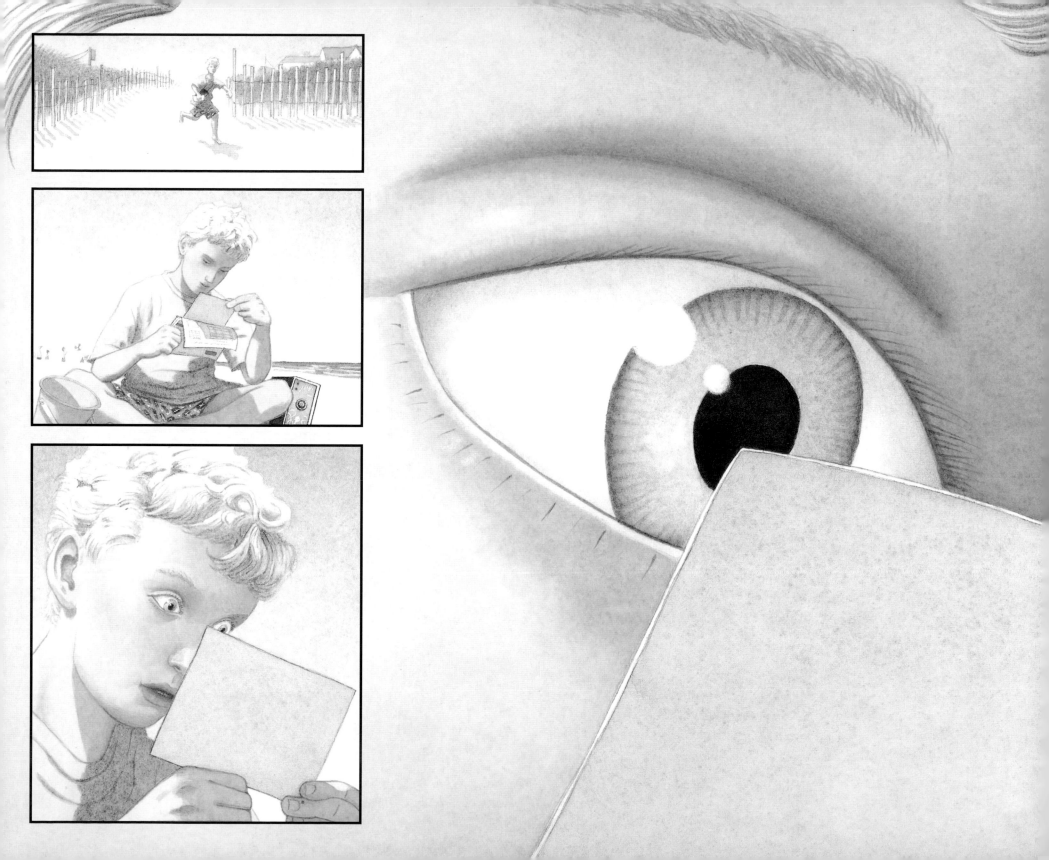

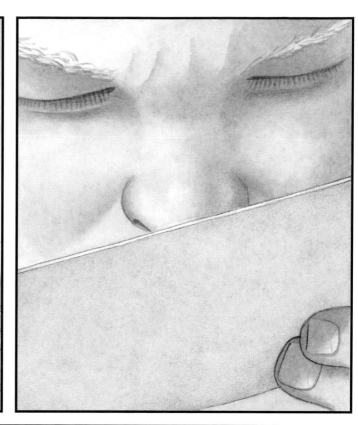

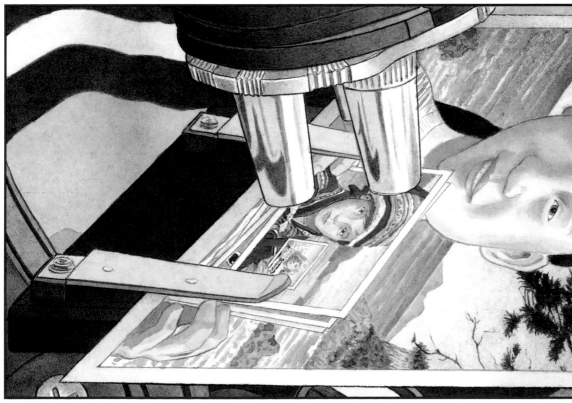

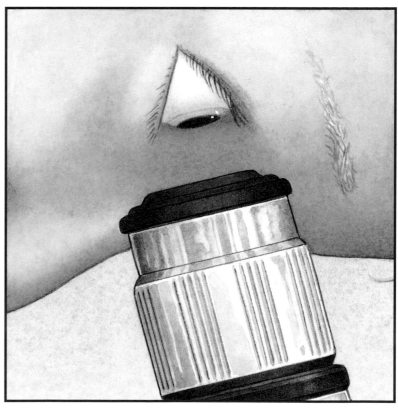

10x

25x

40x

55x

70x

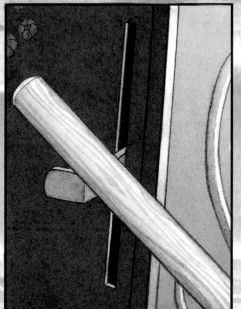

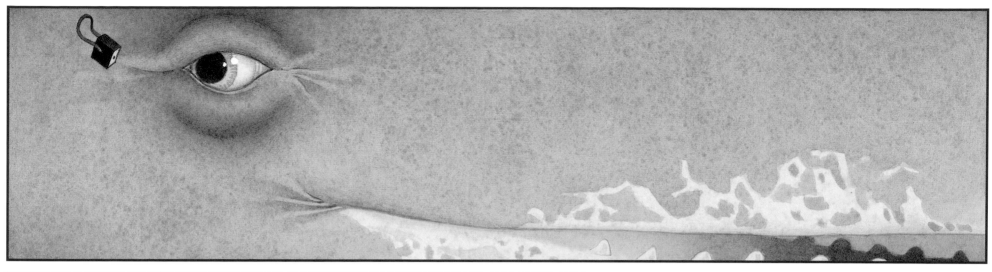

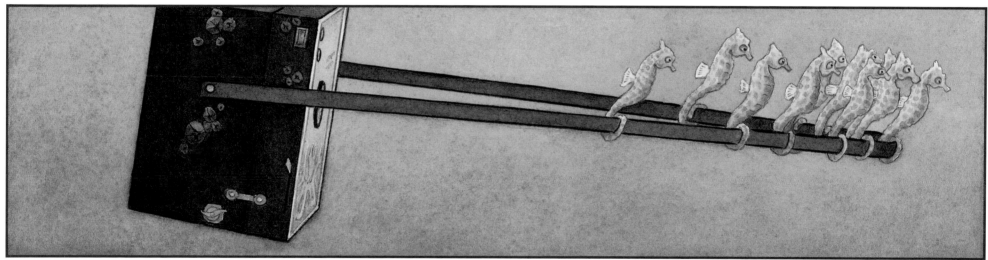

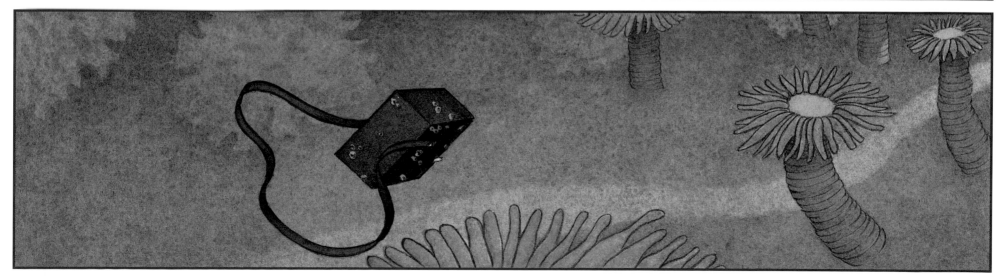